To Brodie Nakia, our cosmic gift . . .
and to Rickey, our angel of light.
—R.M.M.

For my father, Mr. Won, who is my sun,
my moon, and my stars.
—A.W.

Library of Congress Cataloging-in-Publication Data
Names: Montez Minor, Rachel, author. | Won, Annie, illustrator.
Title: The sun, the moon, and the stars / Rachel Montez Minor ; illustrated by Annie Won.
Description: First edition. | New York : Crown Books for Young Readers, [2021] | Audience: Ages 3–6. |
Audience: Grades K–1. | Summary: Illustrations and rhyming text celebrate diverse children, their power
to inspire those around them, and the bonds of family and humanity that can never be broken.
Identifiers: LCCN 2021004749 (print) | LCCN 2021004750 (ebook) | ISBN 978-0-593-30937-7 (trade) |
ISBN 978-0-593-30938-4 (lib. bdg.) | ISBN 978-0-593-30939-1 (ebook)
Subjects: CYAC: Stories in rhyme. | Children—Fiction. | Interpersonal relations—Fiction. | Inspiration—
Fiction. Classification: LCC PZ8.3.M777 Su 2021 (print) | LCC PZ8.3.M777 (ebook) | DDC [E]—dc23

The text of this book is set in 17-point Cabrito Didone.
The illustrations in this book were created digitally.

MANUFACTURED IN CHINA
10 9 8 7 6 5 4 3 2
First Edition

by Rachel Montez Minor   illustrated by Annie Won

The Sun, the Moon, and the Stars

Crown Books for Young Readers
New York

You are like the sun . . .
rising every day
with your energy and light.

Just like the sun,
you make light all around
as you grow big and bright.

Whether you're close,
or whether you're far,
your light keeps shining,
wherever you are.

You are like the moon . . .
sometimes full and big,
sometimes new and small.

Just like the moon
makes oceans rise and fall,
your dreams will attract all who you call.

And as the moon circles the earth
day by day,
you are shaped by your family's love,
connected in every way.

You are like the stars in the night sky,
lighting the way for all to see—
even on their darkest night.

And just like the stars,
your glow travels on . . .
and on and on . . .

. . . guiding the people you love
even from far, far,
and beyond.

So . . . remember to gaze up at the sun, the moon, and the stars and soak in their glow.

After all,
you're more like them
than you'll ever know!

Everything in the sky is connected to you. . . .
You are the universe,
and the universe is you!